DANGER DEMON'S COVE

Karen Dolby

Illustrated by Graham Round

Designed by
Graham Round and Brian Robertson

Contents

About this Book

Danger at Demon's Cove is an exciting adventure that takes you on an ancient trail in search of the amazing Demon's Eye Diamond and lost treasure.

Throughout the book, there are lots of tricky puzzles and perplexing problems which you must solve in order to understand the next part of the story.

Look at the pictures carefully and watch out for vital clues and information. Sometimes you will need to flick back through the book to help you find an answer. There are extra clues on page 41 and you can check the answers on pages 42 to 48.

Just turn the page to begin the adventure . . .

Max

Sally

Max and Sally are on holiday. They are camping outside their grandparents' house on the cliff top above Demon's Cove. Between them, they manage to find all the clues and solve the mystery. Can you?

A Dark and Stormy Night

It was a dark and stormy night, long ago. A ship called the Indian Queen was on her way home from the East, loaded with spices and silk. There was also a secret cargo belonging to a fabulously rich prince which Captain T. Clipper had pledged to guard with his life – an amazing hoard of treasure, including the Demon's Eye, a huge, priceless, black diamond.

The Indian Queen was lashed by fierce waves. The Captain struggled to steer the ship and desperately looked out for the lighthouse beam.

Meanwhile, the three evil Grabbitt brothers waited on the cliffs above Demon's Cove, sending a false signal to lure the ship onto the rocks.

The Captain spotted the signal. The doomed Indian Queen unwittingly sailed onto the treacherous rocks and began sinking fast.

Denzil, Jago and Joshua Grabbitt eagerly hauled the cargo onto the shore, without a thought for the crew of the wrecked ship.

The Indian Queen sank without trace, while the brothers inspected their booty. Denzil, the most evil of them, prised open the chests.

The greedy Grabbitts stared incredulously at the glittering jewels and amazing treasure, hardly able to believe their luck at such a haul.

Tom paused and gazed out to sea. Sally shivered. She could picture it all clearly.

"But what happened to the treasure?" asked Max. "What did the Grabbitts do with it?"

"It's said that they hid the two treasure chests in the maze of smugglers' tunnels at Demon's Cove," Tom continued. "But within months the brothers had mysteriously perished and the secret of the treasure was lost with them.

Some say the Demon's Eye diamond held a curse. No one knows for sure. But even now, ghostly cries are heard echoing through the caves and on stormy nights the phantom Indian Queen can be seen sailing in the bay at Demon's Cove."

Flashing Lights

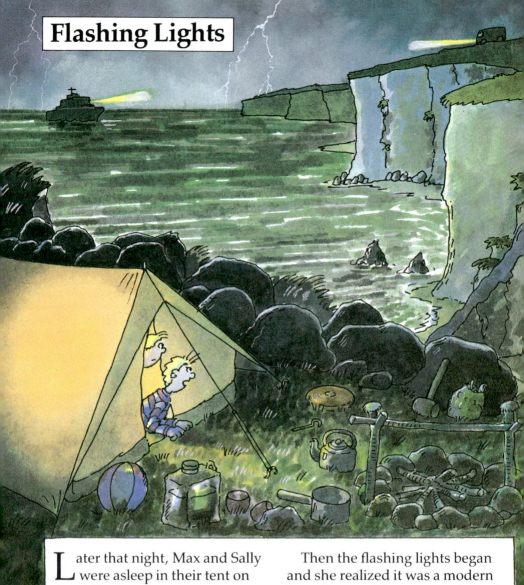

Later that night, Max and Sally were asleep in their tent on the cliffs above Demon's Cove. A sudden loud roar of thunder woke Sally with a start.

She peered out through the tent flap as lightning lit up the bay. Sally rubbed her eyes in disbelief. Was this the ghostly Indian Queen . . . ?

Then the flashing lights began and she realized it was a modern boat. By now Max was awake and they watched as a series of long and short flashes beamed across the bay.

"Perhaps it's a signal," said Max, as a lorry drew up on the cliff top opposite.

Sally quickly grabbed a notebook and started to scribble down the sequence, using dots for short flashes and dashes for long flashes. Max rummaged through a bag stuffed with useful equipment and pulled out his pocket codebook. He flicked through it until he found the page he was looking for and handed it to Sally.

"This will help us work out what it means," he said.

DON'T TURN THE PAGE YET

Can you decode the signal?

Morse Alphabet

A ·—
B —···
C —·—·
D —··
E ·
F ··—·
G ——·
H ····
I ··
J ·———

K —·—
L ·—··
M ——
N —·
O ———
P ·——·
Q ——·—
R ·—·
S ···
T —

U ··—
V ···—
W ·——
X —··—
Y —·——
Z ——··

mistake ······

full stop ·—·—·—

question mark ··——··   end of message ·—·—·

Semaphore

7

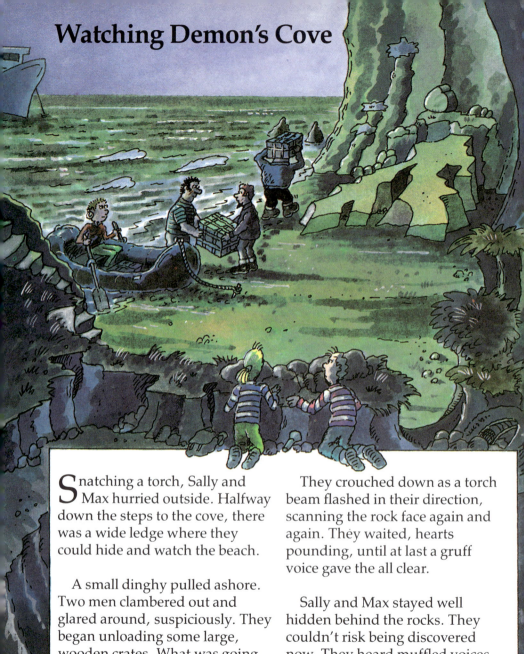

Watching Demon's Cove

Snatching a torch, Sally and Max hurried outside. Halfway down the steps to the cove, there was a wide ledge where they could hide and watch the beach.

A small dinghy pulled ashore. Two men clambered out and glared around, suspiciously. They began unloading some large, wooden crates. What was going on? Were they smugglers? Max leant out to get a better look and dislodged an avalanche of stones and pebbles.

They crouched down as a torch beam flashed in their direction, scanning the rock face again and again. They waited, hearts pounding, until at last a gruff voice gave the all clear.

Sally and Max stayed well hidden behind the rocks. They couldn't risk being discovered now. They heard muffled voices fading into the distance, but could see nothing. Soon there was silence and, in spite of the cold, they both felt very sleepy...

Max woke suddenly, sunlight dazzling him. He jumped to his feet, but the people and dinghy had vanished. He shook Sally and dashed down to the beach.

Max thought he caught a glimpse of the boat, but Sally was puzzled by the footprints. She could see three sets of tracks heading in one direction towards the cliff where they stopped. Someone must have rowed the dinghy away, but where had the other three people gone?

Sally stared at the cliff face, looking for a clue. She thought back to last night. Something had changed.

DON'T TURN THE PAGE YET

What has Sally noticed?

Message in a Bottle

Sally stared up towards the large boulder, sure it was hiding something. She took a deep breath and jumped onto the rocks. She scrambled up to the wide, grassy ledge with Max struggling behind.

Sally leant against the boulder and pushed. It was surprisingly light and rolled away to reveal a narrow opening. Max peered into the gloomy darkness. Sally flicked on the torch and they stepped cautiously through the gap to investigate.

They found themselves in a small cave. The torch beam disturbed some bats, but otherwise the cave was empty. Footprints in the sand matched the ones on the beach and showed that three people had walked into, but not out of, the cave. So where had they gone?

"Perhaps there's a secret tunnel," said Max.

Sally began tapping the walls, but they felt disappointingly solid. Max looked for hidden levers or buttons. But they found nothing.

Suddenly, Sally spotted a block of stone that had been firmly wedged into the wall. After a lot of tugging and a final wrench that sent Max tumbling backwards, they pulled it free and stared into the hole at an old, cobwebby bottle. Sally lifted it from its hiding place and Max pulled out a crumbly roll of paper. It was torn at the edges and faded by damp and age, but they could still see the clear outlines of a map and peculiar, sloping writing that was almost impossible to read.

DON'T TURN THE PAGE YET

Can you work out what the writing says?

Tricky Trapdoor

Sally studied the paper, thinking hard about what it meant. This was only part of a map and she wondered what had happened to the rest of it. She was sure the map was important, why else would Jago Grabbitt have hidden it so carefully? Could it have something to do with the treasure from the Indian Queen?

Max scuffed his way across the floor, searching for signs of a trapdoor. Suddenly he caught his foot in a ring half buried in the ground and tripped, knocking over a heavy, metal pole. He lay sprawled on the floor, but at least he knew where the trapdoor was.

Just then, Sally noticed an unusual, carved stick lying on a rock. She tucked it into her bag, then began to help Max brush away the sand from a heavy, old, oak door.

The rusty, metal ring was embedded in one side of the trapdoor. Max lifted up the ring and tugged.

Together, Sally and Max heaved, pulled and yanked, but still they couldn't lift it. The door wouldn't budge.

They gave up, this was getting them nowhere. There HAD to be another way of opening the trapdoor. Max gazed around the cave searching for inspiration, but there didn't seem to be anything that would help. Then he had a brainwave.

"This should be easy," Max exclaimed, confidently. "I know how to open it."

DON'T TURN THE PAGE YET

How can they open the trapdoor?

Into the Smugglers' Tunnels

Eek! It's dark down here.

I know, stupid. Hurry up and find the torch.

Sally stepped onto the rickety ladder and began to clamber down. Max followed gingerly. But just at that moment, the ladder wobbled. CRASH! The trapdoor slammed shut, plunging them into darkness. They were trapped and had no choice but to go on.

At the bottom, Sally flicked on her torch. The beam barely pierced the blackness. They tried to match their route with Jago's map, but before long they were hopelessly lost.

On and on, they crawled and climbed through dank, dripping tunnels and echoing, shadowy caves. Sometimes they thought they could hear voices, but they saw no one. At last, Max saw a steep flight of steps leading up to a small trapdoor. It creaked as they pushed against it, but opened easily.

As she peered out, Sally gasped, "I know where we are."

DON'T TURN THE PAGE YET

Where are Max and Sally?

The Mystery Thickens

Silence. The cottage was deserted. Max and Sally pushed open the trapdoor and scrambled out.

They gazed at the cluttered room. Every corner and shelf was crammed with an odd assortment of curios collected from around the world. But there were also several puzzling things that seemed very unlikely possessions for a fisherman like Tom.

Suddenly, something made Sally stop and stare, a name she remembered from Tom's story of the Indian Queen.

DON'T TURN THE PAGE YET

What has Sally spotted?

The Old Sea Chest

Max tried the chest. It was unlocked. Sally looked doubtful; she didn't like the idea of snooping through someone else's things.

"There's something going on, and I want to find out what," said Max.

The chest was packed with mementoes from the Indian Queen – the Captain's logbook, ancient charts and old doubloons and pieces of eight . . . Max tried out the telescope, but it didn't work. He just stared into luminous, inky, blackness.

Then a recent newspaper cutting caught his eye. Max was certain he had seen the man in the photo before. He racked his brains trying to remember where.

As he read and reread the stories, a worrying suspicion began to grow in his mind. Everything that had happened started to make sense.

DON'T TURN THE PAGE YET

Where has Max seen the man before? What does he suspect?

Ship's Log (diary)

Nov. 10th. Took on freshe water and supplyes. Our scurvey sufferers seeme greatly cheered. A fayre wind is behinde us and full sails are set. Offered two guineas reward for first sight of lande.

Nov. 11th. Made goode speed during the night, but now the barometer is falling and the wind has changed to a Sou' Westerly direction. We are in for a blow. The crewe seeme cheerfull and long to be home.

Nov 12th. Barometer still fallyng. Have battened downe the hatches and furled the mainsail. Never have I felte

suche a gale, nor seene suche waves. Doubled the men's grog rationes to keep them in goode spirits.

Nov. 13th. Weather still worseninge. Bosun Smollett sighted lande firste, but 'tis an evill night. I feare he will never collect his two guineas, nore will we see our homes againe.

All is lost, we are wrecked. The shippe is being torn apart. I must secure my speciall charge.... Place one's eye to the eye-piece, where the eye shall see nowt but the Eye.

FREE AGAIN

From our man in Cairo

Two members of the notorious Doppel Gang were released yesterday without charge, following the reappearance of the famous six-toed Lost Idol.

They are Gloria Goldfinger, jet-setter and collector of expensive jewellery, and John Smith, alias Luigi Macaroni, Hans Sauerkraut and other names – a ruthless master of disguise.

Both wore dark glasses and John sported a new beard, as they boarded a private plane last night with top lawyer, Eustace Whimpe, bound for an unknown destination.

DARING HELICOPTER JAILBREAK

At dawn this morning, another member of the Doppel Gang, Silas 'Spikey' Scarface, was airlifted from Turnquay prison where he

was serving a sentence for tax evasion. Other prisoners looked on spellbound as the helicopter hovered overhead and Spikey was hoisted by rope from the roof. As yet, there is no clue to his whereabouts.

DAILY SCOOP COMMENT

Could these two events be connected? The Doppel Gang, led by the infamous Baron Grabbitt, is suspected of masterminding numerous robberies, involving ancient gold, jewels and art treasures. So far, Gang members have avoided arrest for any of these crimes. The Doppel Gang is rumoured to have a new mission and to be on the trail of an amazing lost treasure. Baron Grabbitt, questioned at his country residence, Grabbitt Hall, refused to comment but described himself as being on "family business".

Tom Acts Suspiciously

THUD THUD THUD...

Sally and Max slowly repacked the chest, their heads buzzing with unanswered questions.

Had they been watching the infamous Doppel Gang at Demon's Cove last night? Was the Gang searching for the lost treasure from the Indian Queen? And what was Tom's part in all this? It was very suspicious.

Heavy footsteps came closer and closer until they stopped outside the front door. Sally and Max watched in horror as the handle slowly turned. What should they do now? Max scooted into the open trapdoor. Sally shut the chest and dived behind the sofa, hardly daring to breathe as Tom sat down in it. She was trapped.

The silence was broken by a strange, crackling sound, followed by a high-pitched whine. Sally cautiously peeped out over the sofa as Tom leapt to his feet and rushed across to the radio.

He sat down at his desk, adjusted the radio and listened intently through the headphones. He was writing something down and seemed to be checking a notebook.

Max opened the trapdoor and saw a carved stick drop to the floor. It was the same size and just like the one Sally had picked up.

Minutes, later the door banged shut and Tom's brisk footsteps faded into the distance. Sally and Max emerged from hiding.

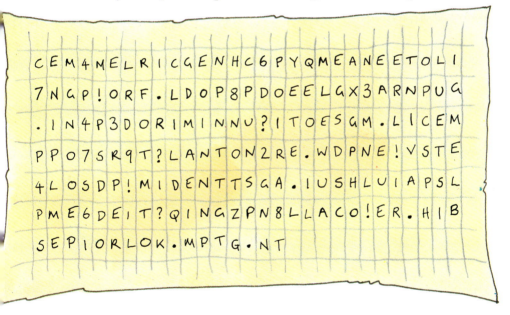

```
C E M 4 M E L R I C G E N H C 6 P Y Q M E A N E E T O L I
7 N G P ! O R F . L D O P 8 P D O E E L G X 3 A R N P U G
. I N 4 P 3 D O R I M I N N U ? I T O E S G M . L I C E M
P P O 7 S R 9 T ? L A N T O N 2 R E . W D P N E ! V S T E
4 L O S D P ! M I D E N T T S G A . I U S H L U I A P S L
P M E 6 D E I T ? Q I N G Z P N 8 L L A C O ! E R . H I B
S E P I O R L O K . M P T G . N T
```

The paper Tom had been writing on was lying on his desk next to the radio. He had neatly written seven rows of letters on the squared paper, but they didn't appear to mean anything. Sally was totally puzzled.

"It's a code," said Max. "And I know how to read it."

DON'T TURN THE PAGE YET

What does the message say?

Looking for X

The message confirmed their worst suspicions, but where WAS the usual meeting place? Max slumped down into a chair. All their detective work seemed to have come to nothing.

Then Sally spotted Tom's notebook lying on top of the radio. It was open at a map marked with a red cross. Could this be the meeting place? It was a long shot, but it had to be worth trying. It was their only lead.

There were no labels, but Sally was sure it was a map of Nether Muckle. She and Max ran outside to the back of the cottage and stared at the village. If only they could match the map to the roads and buildings.

DON'T TURN THE PAGE YET

Can you work out which building is the one marked X on the map?

23

The House on the Cliff Top

Max and Sally sprinted through the village and ran on along the cliff road, past the Smuggler's Head Hotel and ruined abbey. Finally, they turned into the lane leading to the strange house on the cliff's edge.

The steep hill in front of the house made a good viewpoint. Max and Sally scrambled to the top using the thick gorse bushes as cover. Gasping for breath, they crawled to the edge and stared down at Grabbitt Hall, home of Baron Grabbitt. If this was the meeting place, they had to get inside, but finding a way in would be tricky.

DON'T TURN THE PAGE YET

Can you find a safe route into Grabbitt Hall?

GRABBITT HALL

24

Inside Grabbitt Hall

G rabbitt Hall was ominously quiet. Max and Sally sneaked downstairs and along a deserted corridor. Now they had to find out where the meeting was being held, without being discovered.

Max and Sally heard the buzz of voices ahead. They ducked behind a large suit of armour and peered out. A man was standing in the hallway giving directions to two familiar-looking people.

They waited impatiently for the man to walk slowly away down a flight of stairs and then silently tiptoed after the two visitors. Sally and Max turned into a wide, blue-carpeted corridor in time to see them disappearing through a doorway.

A minute later, Max turned the doorhandle and peeped into the room. It was empty. He looked for a door or passage, but the only door was this one. It was very strange, there HAD to be another way out. The two visitors couldn't have vanished into thin air.

The portraits are labelled:

DENZIL GRABBITT · JOSHUA GRABBITT · JAGO GRABBITT · WORZEL GRABBITT · ROBIN GRABBITT
JEAN-PAUL GRABBE À LOTTE · EBENEZER GRABBITT · ABIGAIL GRABBITT · GORDON III BARON · SHEILA GRABBITT
HORATIO II BARON AND ESMERALDA IN THE DRAWING ROOM
JASPER I BARON · GRIZELDA GRABBITT · BRIAN IV BARON

Sally looked around. The walls were covered with portraits of the Baron's Grabbitt ancestors. But something was puzzling Max. Looking at one of the paintings, he could see the room had hardly changed over the years, but one thing was different. What was it?

"I've got it," Max exclaimed. "There's a secret passage, and I know where it is."

DON'T TURN THE PAGE YET

What has Max spotted? Where is the door to the secret passage?

27

The Round Room

Max stood face to face with the portrait of Baron Grabbitt.

"He's not very friendly," he muttered, wondering how to open the door.

Then he saw that one of the Baron's rings had a button where the jewel should have been.

There was a loud whirring as Max touched the button. The Baron slid slowly aside to reveal an eerie, wood-panelled passage, lit only by candlelight. There was no one around, so Max and Sally tiptoed in, not knowing what, or who, to expect. It was a bit spooky, but they reached the open door at the end, unchallenged.

They peeped into a deserted room. Sally glanced around nervously. Where had the two visitors gone? She spotted some scattered papers and part of an ancient-looking map on the table.

"Property of Den . . . it must be Denzil Grabbitt," Sally exclaimed, reading the bottom line of writing.

She delved into her rucksack and pulled out Jago's map. She knew it would match Denzil's. Max whipped out his new, mini camera. CLICK and the picture was taken.

"Now we've got a copy of the map and no one will know we've been here," he said, stuffing the camera into his pocket. "Let's go."

Sally was looking at the map. There was still one piece missing, but she was sure the writing would give them a clue to where the treasure was hidden.

The writing on Denzil's map was very strange, but as she stared it began to make sense.

DON'T TURN THE PAGE YET

What is written on the map?

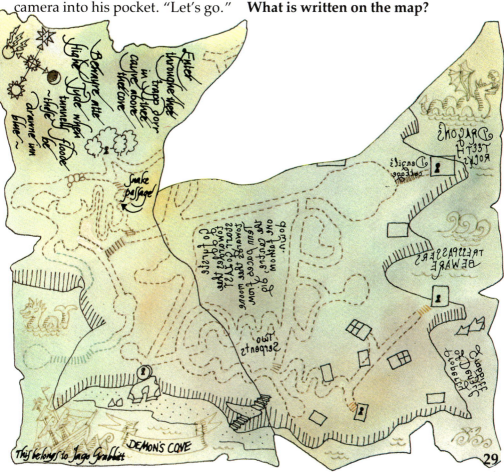

Trapped

There was an ominous scraping sound. A panel opened revealing another room and gloomy passage. Framed in the doorway stood Baron Grabbitt and the Doppel Gang.

"I'll take that," the Baron snarled, snatching the map from Max. "We've been watching you sneaking through the Hall on the TV screen."

Max groaned. Closed circuit television; they should have guessed. He looked around, but they were surrounded with no hope of escape. Sally watched miserably as the lady with orange hair studied their map. At least they still had the camera and film. Spikey grabbed Max and a man called Harry pushed Sally towards the dark passage.

They were marched down a flight of wide, stone stairs and through a huge cave to a long passageway. Harry hurried them straight on, ignoring the tunnels on either side, until they came to seven steep steps.

At the bottom they turned left and carried on into a small, round cave. Even Sally had to duck as she stepped into the low tunnel that twisted down and down. There were more steps, but these were so wet and slippery that Sally, who was trying to memorize their route, lost count.

Finally they came to a small, damp cave where the two men left them tied up. Max wriggled across to some jagged rocks and began to saw at the rope around his wrists. Luckily, it was easy to cut. Meanwhile, Sally had worked out where they were and was trying to find the best route out of the caves, avoiding Grabbitt Hall. Her brilliant memory meant she could picture the map clearly.

DON'T TURN THE PAGE YET

Where are they? Which is the shortest route out, avoiding Grabbitt Hall?

Escape through the Tunnels

Sally and Max ran so quickly, they were gasping for breath by the time they reached the Snake Passage. But at least there was no danger of being followed here. The tunnel was so narrow, it was a tight squeeze even for Max and Sally.

At last they came to a wider passage which sloped steeply upwards towards a small wooden door. But as Max fumbled with the catch, they heard footsteps, running. A tall figure loomed suddenly from the dark shadows behind them.

"I thought I'd never catch you," a gruff voice wheezed.

Tom! They were trapped. Max shoved against the door, trying desperately to open it. Then Tom whisked out a plastic identity card.

"We thought…" Sally began.

". . . I was one of the Doppel Gang," Tom finished. "I realized that. I came to rescue you and guessed you would make for here, but I had to go the long way round."

They set off at once for Tom's cottage where he could develop their film. As they scrambled out and made their way through the wood and across the fields, Tom told them the rest of the story.

The Grabbitts made an ingenious plan to hide the treasure until the hunt for it had been called off.

They hid it in the confusing maze of tunnels at Demon's Cove and drew a map to show the hiding place.

But the brothers didn't trust each other so they divided the map into three parts. Each wrote a vital clue on his portion. When they died, the map was forgotten.

I'm very interested in the case of the Indian Queen treasure, as Captain Clipper is my great great great grandfather.

Baron Grabbitt is Denzil's great great grandson. Gloria Goldfinger discovered Denzil's map while going through some of his old books.

I have been trailing the Gang for months, investigating their activities.

This is how the Doppel Gang's hunt for the treasure and for the missing parts of the map began.

Photo Identification

Tom led Sally and Max into a tumbledown barn behind his cottage. They gazed around in amazement. Inside, the barn was transformed into a high-tech office. Tom opened an important-looking box marked "Police File". It was packed with photographs.

"I want you to help with evidence," Tom explained, making Max and Sally feel very important. "Pick out every photo showing members of the Doppel Gang."

Tom disappeared into the darkroom with their film while Max and Sally spread out the photos. He particularly wanted them to identify the two new gang members. At first it seemed impossible, but they soon spotted familiar faces and some which were cleverly disguised. They could also name most of them.

DON'T TURN THE PAGE YET

Find all the photos of the Doppel Gang and name as many as you can.

The Missing Link

Tom studied the photos of the two new Gang members and frowned.

"Fingers Golightly and Dinah Might. Notorious villains," he said.

Tom held out the newly-developed print showing the two portions of the treasure map. He locked the barn and led Sally and Max across the garden towards his cottage.

As he opened the back door, all three heard a suspicious, scuffling noise.

They were just in time to see a man disappear through the front door.

Tom glanced across at his safe. It was open and he knew it was empty.

Sally dashed to the window and saw Spikey running towards a van. He was brandishing a small piece of paper. The engine revved, Spikey jumped inside and the van roared away.

Tom lifted down a dusty tin.

"The Doppel Gang must know who I am," he said. "They've taken my copy. But . . . I've still got the original."

Copy? Original? What was Tom talking about? He took a small scrap of yellowing paper from the tin. It was the third piece of the Grabbitt brothers' map.

"But how did you find it?" asked Sally, not quite believing her eyes.

This portion of the map had belonged to Joshua Grabbitt, the youngest of the brothers. For Tom was not only descended from Captain Clipper, but also from Joshua Grabbitt. The Captain's grandson had married Joshua's grandaughter. Just last week, Tom had found the map rolled up and forgotten in the attic along with Captain Clipper's chest. Now they could work out where the treasure was hidden. But they would have to move fast to get there before the Doppel Gang.

DON'T TURN THE PAGE YET

Can you work out where the treasure is hidden?

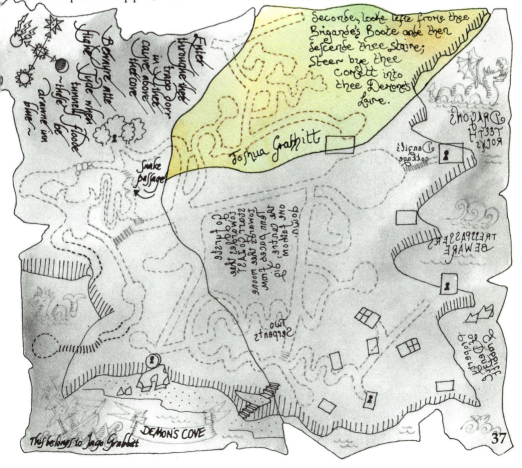

Treasure from the Indian Queen

They raced out to Tom's jeep and set off. Tom radioed for reinforcements and the jeep lurched down the gravel track. With Max in the lead, they scrambled through the trapdoor and down into the maze of dark tunnels, to the Demon's Lair. The Doppel Gang had yet to arrive.

Large boulders made a screen around one side of the cave. It was impossible to hear anyone approaching because it was high tide and the sound of the sea roaring in the tunnels echoed through the cave. Tom found a good hiding place where they could keep watch. They switched off their torch and waited.

It was not long before Max spotted a torch beam. The Doppel Gang marched into the cave. Harry counted ten paces from the centre and the Gang set to work with spades, while Gloria and the Baron watched.

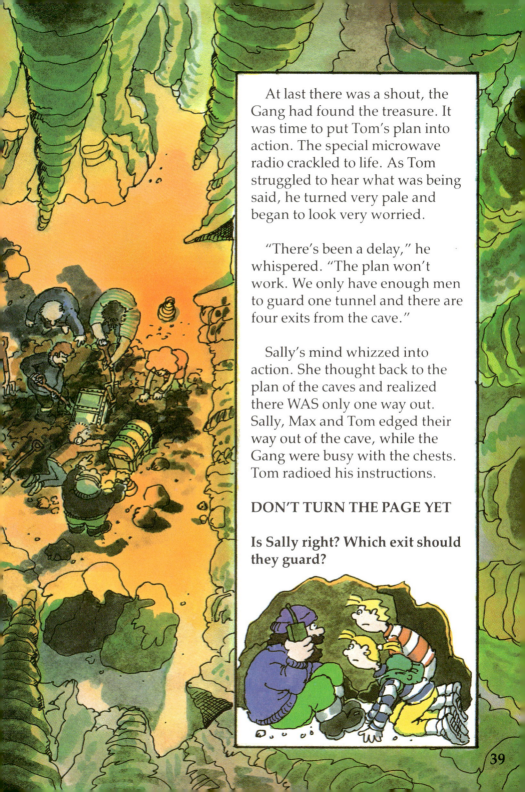

At last there was a shout, the Gang had found the treasure. It was time to put Tom's plan into action. The special microwave radio crackled to life. As Tom struggled to hear what was being said, he turned very pale and began to look very worried.

"There's been a delay," he whispered. "The plan won't work. We only have enough men to guard one tunnel and there are four exits from the cave."

Sally's mind whizzed into action. She thought back to the plan of the caves and realized there WAS only one way out. Sally, Max and Tom edged their way out of the cave, while the Gang were busy with the chests. Tom radioed his instructions.

DON'T TURN THE PAGE YET

Is Sally right? Which exit should they guard?

The Demon's Eye Diamond

The plan was a success. Almost before Max and Sally knew it, the six members of the Doppel Gang were safely in police custody. Tom, Max and Sally followed as the Gang were led through the tunnels to Demon's Cove, where a police launch was waiting. Outside on the beach, Tom opened the chests. Max and Sally gazed in amazement at the treasure. But they quickly realized something was wrong. The red leather box that should have held the Demon's Eye diamond was empty.

Had one of the Doppel Gang secretly taken it? Sally didn't think so. She was convinced the Grabbitt brothers had never found the famous jewel all those years ago. But if she was right, where was it now? Sally remembered Captain Clipper's logbook, she knew that it held the answer.

DON'T TURN THE PAGE YET

Where is the Demon's Eye diamond?

Clues

Pages 6-7

Look at Max's codebook. Each group of dots and dashes stands for a letter.

Pages 8-9

This is easy. Use your eyes.

Pages 10-11

The letters are written in old-fashioned English. Some words are spelt strangely.

Pages 12-13

Look carefully at all the things in the cave.

Pages 14-15

Look back through the book. Do you recognize anything?

Pages 16-17

This is easy. Use your eyes.

Pages 18-19

Look back at the people on page 8.

Pages 20-21

The carved stick Sally picked up on page 12 will help.

Pages 22-23

Try turning the map the other way up. Work out where Tom's cottage is first.

Pages 24-25

They can crawl behind bushes and walls to keep out of sight. Are there any open windows or doors?

Pages 26-27

This is easy. Compare the room as it is now to the same room shown in one of the paintings.

Pages 28-29

The clues on this page give you a clue to Denzil's writing.

Pages 30-31

Look back at the two pieces of map. Grabbit Hall was built on the site of Denzil's cottage.

Pages 34-35

Use your eyes and remember what you have learnt about members of the Doppel Gang.

Pages 36-37

Look at all the clues on the map and try putting them into order.

Pages 38-39

You may need to look back at the map on the previous page.

Page 40

Carefully read Captain Clipper's logbook on page 19.

Answers

Pages 6-7

The message is in morse code. This is what it says:

Diving party landing with equipment and wreckage from Indian Queen. Standby to receive at Demon's Cove. End of message.

Pages 8-9

One thing has changed. The large boulder on top of the ledge has been turned round. It is ringed in both pictures.

Large boulder

Pages 10-11

The letters are written in an old-fashioned way and where the letter s comes in the middle of a word, it is written like an f. Some words are also spelt differently.
This is what it says:

Enter through the trapdoor in the cave above the Cove.

This keyhole symbol shows there is a door.

Beware at high tide when tunnels flood – they be drawn in blue.

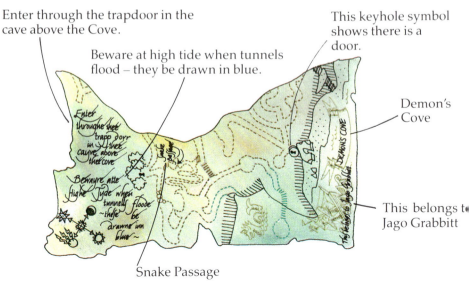

Demon's Cove

This belongs to Jago Grabbitt

Snake Passage

Pages 12-13

They open the trapdoor using the metal pole Max knocked over as a lever. They balance the pole on top of the rock which then acts as a pivot.

The pole is pushed through the ring

Metal pole lever

Pivot rock

This means they need less effort and strength to open the door.
These diagrams show how Max and Sally open the trapdoor.

They push here to lift open the trapdoor

Pages 14-15

The trapdoor opens into Tom's cottage. Sally knows this because she spots the stained glass window which she saw from the outside on page 5.

Stained glass window

Pages 16-17

Sally has spotted the name Captain T. Clipper on the sea chest. He was captain of the Indian Queen. You can see the name ringed here.

The other puzzling things Max and Sally have noticed are labelled.

Gun in holster

Powerful binoculars

Radio transceiver

Camera and lenses

Pistol

Pages 18-19

Max saw the man in the photo last night. He was one of the people on the beach at Demon's Cove.

Here is the man from the photo.

Max suspects the Doppel Gang are looking for the lost treasure from the Indian Queen. His main reasons are: the Doppel Gang's interest in ancient treasure; the message Max and Sally decoded on page 7; the fact that

Baron Grabbitt, the Gang leader, has the same surname as the Grabbitt brothers who wrecked the Indian Queen.

Pages 20-21

Max decodes the message using the carved stick that Sally found on page 12. Place the stick below each line of writing. Lines on the stick match the letters on the paper. To break the code, read the letters which are above notches on the stick.

Here is the message:

Emergency meeting of Doppel Gang in 30 minutes. Important new developments. Usual meeting place. Be prompt.

Pages 22-23

The building marked X on the map is ringed in black.

Tom's cottage is here.

Pages 24-25

The safe route into Grabbitt Hall is marked in black.

Pages 26-27

In the painting above the fireplace, Max spotted a door where the life-size portrait of Baron Grabbitt now hangs. The entrance to the hidden passage must be behind this picture.

This is the door Max spotted.

The door is behind this portrait.

Pages 28-29

The words on Denzil's portion of the map are written backwards. This is what it says:

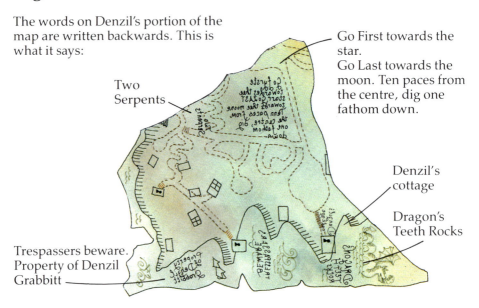

Go First towards the star.
Go Last towards the moon. Ten paces from the centre, dig one fathom down.

Two Serpents

Denzil's cottage

Dragon's Teeth Rocks

Trespassers beware. Property of Denzil Grabbitt

Pages 30-31

The shortest way out is marked in black.

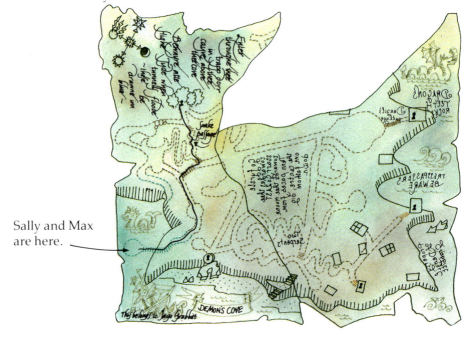

Sally and Max are here.

Pages 34-35

Here you can see the members of the Doppel Gang.

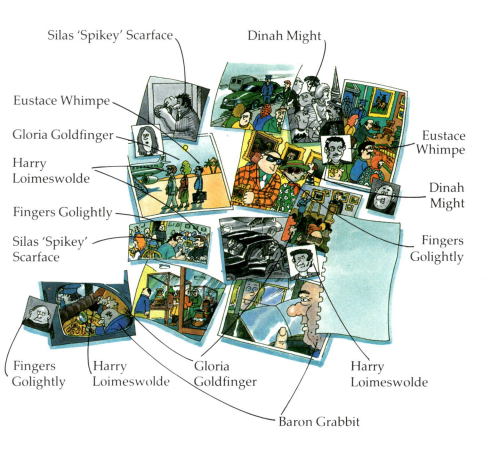

Silas 'Spikey' Scarface

Dinah Might

Eustace Whimpe

Gloria Goldfinger

Harry Loimeswolde

Fingers Golightly

Silas 'Spikey' Scarface

Eustace Whimpe

Dinah Might

Fingers Golightly

Fingers Golightly

Harry Loimeswolde

Gloria Goldfinger

Harry Loimeswolde

Baron Grabbit

Pages 36-37

Written in order, the clues say:
Enter through the trapdoor in the cave above the Cove. (Map page 11.)
Go First towards the star. (Map page 29.)
Second, look left from the Brigand's Boot and then descend the stair; steer by the comet into the Demon's Lair. (Map page 37.)

Go Last towards the moon. Ten paces from the centre, dig one fathom down. (Map page 29.)

(One fathom is equal to six feet.)

You can see where the treasure is buried on the completed map, shown on the next page.

The treasure is buried here.

The Grabbitt brothers' route to the treasure is marked here in black.

Pages 38-39

Sally is right.
This is the only tunnel that must be guarded.

It is high tide and so this tunnel is flooded.

This tunnel is blocked.

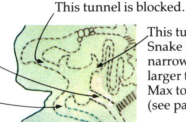

This tunnel leads to the Snake Passage. It is too narrow for anyone larger than Sally and Max to squeeze through (see page 32).

Page 40

Read the last entry in Captain Clipper's logbook on page 19. This tells you the Demon's Eye diamond is hidden in the telescope which Max tries to look through on page 18.

You can see the diamond gleaming here.

SEARCH
FOR THE
SUNKEN CITY

Martin Oliver

Illustrated by Brenda Haw

Designed by Kim Blundell

Edited by Karen Dolby

Contents

About this Story

Search for the Sunken City is a thrilling story in which you pit your wits against a ruthless enemy in a perilous adventure above and below the seas.

Throughout the book, there are lots of tricky puzzles and perplexing problems which you must solve in order to understand the next part of the story.

You may need to flick back through the book to help you find an answer. There are extra clues on page 91 and you can check your answers on pages 92 to 96.

Toby and Flic's adventure began one summer's day when the phone rang. It was Uncle Ollie, the world-famous marine archeologist…

Hello Flic, Toby . . . Great news, I've discovered the wreck of an old galleon . . . I think it's The Dolphin which belonged to the famous explorer, San Miguel Da Silva . . . We've found some incredible things . . . Your holiday should be very exciting . . . Yes, I'll meet you on the beach as arranged.

Toby

Flic

Uncle Ollie

Meeting Uncle Ollie

Toby and Flic scrambled over the rocks to the busy beach. Flic shaded her eyes and looked around. Where was Uncle Ollie?

In the distance they heard the roar of an engine and a whoosh of spray. It was Ollie racing towards the beach in a dinghy.

Ollie jumped ashore, waving to Flic and Toby. He rushed up the beach and led them into his hut.

"Great to see you," he said, emptying out his bag. "I've got some amazing things to show you."

"They're from The Dolphin," explained Ollie, as Toby and Flic gazed at the odd collection of objects.

"Since I discovered the wreck I've been rushed off my flippers," said Ollie, taking Flic and Toby outside.

"I hope these finds will help me solve a mystery that has puzzled explorers for years," he continued.

Flic and Toby leant forward eagerly.

"Let me explain," he began, when suddenly . . .

They dashed inside. The shutters were wide open and the finds from The Dolphin were scattered over the floor.

"It must have been a strong breeze," said Toby.

But it had taken more than a strong breeze to do this. Flic was sure something was missing from the room.

What is missing?

Paper Chase

They raced outside to look for clues. Toby quickly spotted some footprints and a figure sprinting down the beach.

They set off in hot pursuit. Flic yelled out, but the villain only ran faster. Toby and Flic accelerated and began to catch up.

"Who was that?" gasped Toby, picking himself up.

"And why did he steal Da Silva's diary," asked Flic. "Maybe Ollie will know."

Ollie arrived panting and wheezing. As he struggled to get his breath back, he shook his head at their questions. Then he pointed to some scraps of paper lying on the sand.

The thief splashed into the water and jumped aboard a getaway boat. The motor immediately roared into life.

Toby made a despairing dive, but it was too late! He and Flic could only watch as the boat zoomed out to sea.

We landed on the first island in our path and found fresh water, wild goats and plentiful wildfowl. We beached the *Dolphin* there. June 11th. The hull will take months to repair. The crew began building some huts, a windmill and a look-out post ...
Aug 20th. An incredible day !! Have made the most amazing dis-

skull-shaped isle, but it was barren. island. We found water as we rowed and continued our foul, flat island the E... As we landed on the stony isle. Honestly, or... attack. We missed again. to red cross scrawled on it, to seaward, so... some but were

"I saw them fall out of the thief's hand as you chased after him," he explained breathlessly. "If we can fit them together, they might help us find out what the crook was after."

Flic and Toby picked up the scraps. They were covered in old-fashioned handwriting.

What do the scraps of paper say?

55

Ollie Explains

Toby and Flic turned to Uncle Ollie, their heads buzzing with questions. But before they could say anything, Ollie hurried them into the dinghy.

"A chart . . . a chart in a sea chest," he muttered rereading the pieces of Da Silva's diary. "Maybe it's still there. We must search the wreck."

"Hang on a minute," Flic interrupted. "What's going on?"

Ollie smiled and handed over the tiller to Toby. As they sped away from the shore, he began to explain . . . .

Wherever he explored, he left a gift bearing his famous family crest.

The Captain of The Dolphin was San Miguel Da Silva, an intrepid adventurer and explorer. Da Silva sailed all over the world with his trusty crew.

Da Silva returned from his voyages with amazing tales of the strange animals and lands he had seen. The farther he travelled, the stranger his tales became, until no one believed him.

Da Silva's most incredible tale was his discovery of a fabulous sunken city. He claimed it was the mythical city of Mare Vellos.

According to legend, Mare Vellos was the twin city of Phabulos. Both were founded by the famous hero, Hero and shared his lion crest. But Mare Vellos was built of gold and marble and soon exceeded its twin in wealth and power.

Its glory increased until, so the legend says, Mare Vellos was struck by an earthquake and submerged by a tidal wave.

When no one believed his tale, Da Silva set sail to bring back proof of the city but he never returned. The Dolphin was caught in a storm and sank without trace.

Any proof Da Silva raised was lost with him. Since then many people have searched for the city, but in vain. The ruins of Phabulos were found years ago, but Da Silva's story of his discovery has been discounted as a hoax until now . . .

The Jolly Dodger

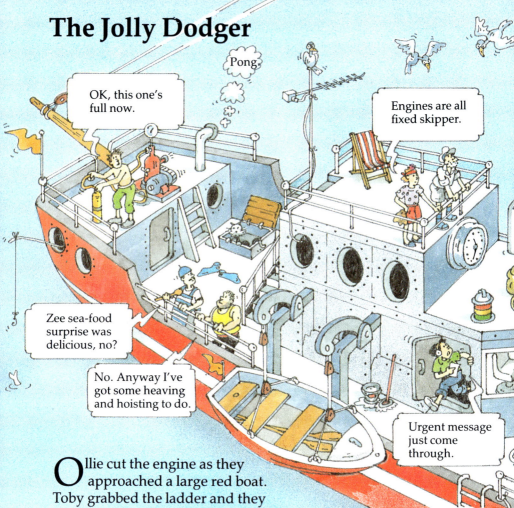

Ollie cut the engine as they approached a large red boat. Toby grabbed the ladder and they all scrambled aboard.

"I hired everything myself," Ollie stated proudly, as Toby and Flic stared round at the ramshackle diving gear and the motley crew.

"Time to get kitted up for diving," said Ollie, excitedly. "But only one of you can come down with me. We're short of air and one experienced diver."

Toby and Flic looked glumly at each other. They both wanted to explore the wreck. Flic peered over Ollie's shoulder at the papers in his dive file.

As she listened to the crew, she realized that she and Toby could both dive and she knew who with.

Who can they dive with?
What about the air cylinders?

58

Diving on The Dolphin

Flic held onto her facemask and stepped off the ladder. Air bubbles whooshed and burst over her. She quickly ran through her equipment checks, trying to remember her diving lessons.

Then she slowly swam down to join the others. They finned over a mudbank and through a shoal of silvery fish. Toby brushed his way through a patch of sinewy seaweeds and suddenly breathed out a long stream of bubbles. Ahead lay The Dolphin.

The ship was broken in two and covered in floating fronds and barnacles. Michelle led the search and began to explore the hull. Toby peered around and out of the corner of his eye, he spotted it . . . The very thing they were looking for!

What has Toby seen?

The Sea Chest

Ollie noted the position of the chest on his site plan while the others attached a buoy to it. The four divers swam to the surface while the chest floated gently upwards.

They bobbed up and down in the swell then scrambled onto the deck of The Jolly Dodger. Toby took off his mask and watched excitedly as the chest was hoisted aboard.

It was Da Silva's chest. But did it contain his chart? Ollie picked the lock with his trusty skeleton key and tugged at the lid. Nothing happened.

It was jammed shut. Ollie tried again, this time with Flic's help. They pushed and pulled until suddenly the lid sprang open, sending them flying.

Toby stared into the chest half expecting to find it packed with ancient treasure. But the chest was empty, except for a musty smell and a roll of paper. Ollie studied it carefully. It was Da Silva's chart.

"These are the Sardonic islands, only two days' sail from here," he exclaimed. "Our next move towards the city, is to work out where Da Silva set up his base."

Where was Da Silva's island base?

A Mysterious Message

Two days later, Toby and Flic were taking first watch with Uncle Ollie. Dawn was breaking and the crew were asleep.

"Keep your eyes peeled," Ollie said. "You should see the island at any minute."

Toby and Flic scanned the horizon. Suddenly Toby's ears pricked up as he heard a whirr and a crackle of static from the radio room.

"No one should be using the radio at this time," he said. "Come on, let's investigate."

Toby motioned to Flic to follow him and tiptoed towards the radio room trying hard not to make a sound.

CLANG. He stepped on a bar of soap, skidded along the deck and crashed into a bucket and mop.

As Flic helped him to his feet, Toby thought he caught a glimpse of a shadowy figure sprinting towards the crew's quarters.

But before he could speak, Flic put her finger to her mouth and pointed to the radio room. The door was ajar and a light was shining under it.

They pulled the door open and cautiously peered in. The room was empty, but the radio was switched on and set to receive. Who had been using it? And what message had they received?

Flic noticed that the top sheet of the radio operator's pad had been hurriedly torn off.

This gave Toby an idea. Whoever received the message must have written it down on the pad. He picked up a pencil and scribbled on the top sheet of the pad. The imprint of a message appeared, but it was in code.

Can you work out what the message says?

AVL ISADYB NE DDIHS EU
LCDN AEGAS SEMLA
TIVADN IF LLLWYEH
TES IWRE HTO "SECRO
FLARU TANY BN EVIRDS ID
NIMD EISI WTT UOB ATNEM
UCODLAGELA" ER EH WEC
AL PEHTT AHC RA EST ON
TAEP ERTO NISU MMIH
HTI WSTA RBOWT EH
TD NAREV ILO

Land Ahoy

Just then, Ollie's cry of "Land Ahoy!" echoed around The Jolly Dodger. Toby and Flic raced up to the bridge and spotted their destination – Da Silva's island dead ahead.

Instructions rang out and there was a mad scramble as the crew raced about the decks. They loaded up a strange assortment of small boats and headed towards the island.

Ollie scrambled into a boat with Toby and Flic. As he rowed for shore, Flic told him about the coded message. Who had sent it? Was the same person behind the theft of the diary?

This enemy wanted to stop them searching a place on the island. He had described it with a cryptic clue, but where was it?

Where is the place?

Island Trek

As the trio waded ashore, Ollie thought about the crew who were busy setting up camp. One of them must be a spy, but he didn't know who.

Now was their chance to head for the windmill before the spy noticed they were gone. They hurried along a dusty track and scrambled up a steep slope.

The beach was soon left far behind as they raced on into the unknown. They hiked uphill between sharp rocks and prickly bushes. Flic turned a corner…

She gasped. They were standing in an arena. Their path to the windmill was blocked by a large semi-circular amphitheatre looming up in front of them.

Rows of seats were chiselled into the steep cliff. Some had crumbled away completely, leaving sheer rock. There was no way round.

"We'll have to go back," Ollie groaned. "Unless we can find a way up one step at a time."

Can you find a way to the top?

Colour Code

At last they reached the windmill. Toby shivered in spite of the heat. He had the spooky feeling that they were being watched. Ollie glanced at a crumbly wall. His eyes opened wide and he began scrabbling through his rucksack.

"It's incredible," he shouted, pulling out his magnifying glass. "I've found Da Silva's message."

Toby crouched beside Ollie and they stared at a section of the wall. They could clearly make out some words that were chiselled into the stone. Ollie and Toby read them aloud, but they didn't seem to make any sense.

"I'm sure that this is the key to decoding Da Silva's message," said Flic, "Now all we've got to do is find it."

When A becomes M and Z becomes L, my message I will tell. Da Silva.

Start on red, read clockwise, then stop on green and my message will be seen.

The trio split up and began searching the area. They checked inside the windmill, behind columns and even under the stones on the ground, but they found nothing. Ollie slumped down glumly. The trail had run dry.

Just then a sudden gust of wind whistled around the mill. The sails creaked into life, Toby glanced up and spotted words painted onto them.

What does the message say?

Ollie Investigates

Toby groaned at the thought of more clues while Flic scratched her head and stared at the message again. There was something rather odd about it, but Ollie didn't seem to mind.

"I'll look for the clues while you recheck the map and diary fragments," he said, handing them over. "Stay here and wait for me. This won't take long."

Toby and Flic glanced at the chart, but it was too hot. They flopped down in the cool shade and began to snooze.

Meanwhile Ollie scrabbled in the ruins. He brushed away some dust and peered intently at the mosaic he had uncovered.

Toby woke up with a start, feeling very thirsty. He was just about to take a swig from his water bottle when he felt something tickling his leg. He looked down and yelled.

Ollie was still looking for clues when he spotted a marble head. It was Hero, the founder of Mare Vellos. He gently pulled the head out of the wall. Then everything went black…

Toby and Flic were brushing off ants when they heard a crash and a muffled shout. Had something happened to Ollie? They picked up their bags and dashed towards the ruins.

Suddenly Flic stopped dead in her tracks. She saw something that she recognized. Ollie was in trouble!

What has Flic spotted?

Following the Trail

Toby and Flic looked at each other in horror. Where was Ollie? They followed the trail of footprints to the edge of a cliff and looked over. The footprints continued down an almost sheer rock face.

"Let's go," gulped Toby, trying hard not to look down.

They slipped and slid down the steep slope, dodging past spiky thistles and through a swarm of buzzing hornets. Flic skidded to a halt as a scorpion scuttled across their path. Toby tripped, sending an avalanche of stones rattling down. But at last they reached the bottom in one piece.

Toby stared across the bay and ducked for cover when he saw what Flic was pointing at.

THE DIRTY SWAB

Uncle Ollie! He was being hauled onto a yacht by a tough-looking villain.

"We must get aboard that boat and find out what's going on," said Flic.

How? They would be spotted if they tried to swim across the bay, but they could reach the cliff top behind the boat unnoticed.

How can they get aboard the boat?

The Plot Thickens

Toby and Flic leapt from rock to rock and clambered silently onto the deck of the boat. They crept past a snoozing sentry and peered in through a porthole.

"That must be the dastardly crook behind all this," gasped Flic, staring at the tall figure threatening Ollie.

"His name is Dr Schwindler," said Toby, pointing to the passport that was among some papers lying on the table below.

He carefully studied the photos and sheets of paper. Now it was clear why Schwindler was so interested in finding Da Silva's sunken city.

There was a knock on the cabin door. Schwindler hurriedly picked up his plans and locked them in a drawer, uncovering some pieces of Da Silva's diary.

Toby and Flic gasped as a familiar figure walked into the cabin . . . Michelle Silver! She was the spy amongst their crew.

Schwindler turned back to Ollie and tried to force him to reveal the location of the city.

"I know where it is," Toby whispered, reading Schwindler's pieces of the diary. "But first we must rescue Ollie."

Where should they dive?

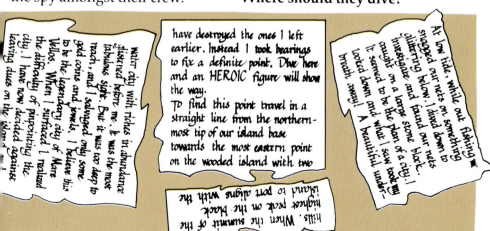

have destroyed the ones I left earlier. Instead I took bearings to fix a definite point. Dive here and an HEROIC figure will show the way.
To find this point travel in a straight line from the northern-most tip of our island base towards the most eastern point on the wooded island with two

water city with riches in abundance glistened before me. It was the most fabulous sight. But it was too deep to reach, and I salvaged only some gold coins and jewels. I believe this to be the legendary city of Mora Vellos. When I surfaced I realized the difficulty of pinpointing the city. I have now decided against leaving clues on the island

At low tide, while out fishing we snagged our nets on something glittering below. I dived down to investigate and found our nets caught on a large stone block. It seemed to be the plan of a city! I looked down and what I saw took my breath away! A beautiful under—

hills. When the summit of the highest peak on the Black island to port aligns with the

77

Captured

Schwindler realized he was getting nowhere with Ollie, and he stormed out of the cabin with Michelle. As soon as the crooks had gone, Toby squirmed and squeezed his way through the porthole. He landed in the cabin with a thud.

They all held their breath. The boat was quiet. No one had heard. Flic wriggled in and dashed over to Ollie.

"Am I glad to see you," Ollie whispered, as Flic wrestled with the knots tying him to the wall. "We must get out of here and stop those villains."

The last rope fell to the ground. Ollie stretched his arms and legs, but Flic froze. Footsteps pounded towards them. They rushed to the porthole, desperate to escape. But it was too late.

The cabin door swung open and they came face to face with the sneering Dr Schwindler and his henchmen.

"Welcome aboard," he hissed. "There will be no way out for you three now."

Before I discover the city, I will pay a visit to your ship.

The evil doctor ordered his sidekick to tie up the trio, then he tipped out their bags. He spotted the map and fragments and grabbed them triumphantly.

"Hah! Now the sunken city is mine," he cackled. "Don't try to escape. Michelle will guard you very closely while I 'research' the treasury."

Schwindler and his crooked crony slammed the door shut. Toby's brain jolted into action. They had to escape and foil Schwindler's plan. But how? If only Michelle wasn't convinced that they were looters.

Suddenly Toby realized there was evidence to prove that Schwindler was the real looter. If only they could get it.

What is the proof?
How can they get it?

Race Against Time

Michelle read Schwindler's plans and needed no more convincing. She quickly untied the others, led them off the deserted boat and into the dinghy.

They soon reached The Jolly Dodger and jumped aboard. The race against Schwindler was on. Michelle started the engines. Following Da Silva's directions, Toby and Flic looked out for the yellow rock and the black peak while Ollie steered a straight course to the dive spot.

If we run into trouble or find anything down there, I will let off this signal flare. Lower your strongest steel net where you see it.

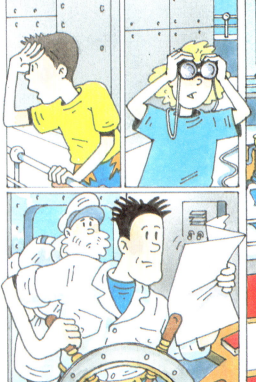

They kitted up in record time and Michelle, Ollie and Toby dived into the sea. Flic scanned the horizon for a sign of Schwindler. She reached for an underwater signal flare and whispered a plan to the captain.

She climbed down the ladder and was about to jump in, when Michelle shot out of the water.

"There's a limpet mine attached to the hull," she spluttered. "And it's timed to go off in four minutes."

"Schwindler designed it," she shouted. "The numbers in each row, column and diagonal add up to 34. The buttons are numbered 1 to 16, but some numbers have rusted away. To defuse the bomb, we must press button number 13. But we have to find it first."

They dived down to the others who were tugging at the bomb. Flic's mind whirred into action as she glanced at the clock. She gulped. Time was running out.

Which button should they press?

Which Way?

Michelle defused the bomb with seconds to spare. It was a narrow escape, but now they must get back to the search for the sunken city.

Ollie led the way as they swam down through the shallow water. Weeds floated in the current and eels darted out of crevices in the jagged coral reefs.

Suddenly Michelle spotted a round object lying on the sea bed. She picked it up and gasped. It was a man's head. Then she realized that it was part of a marble statue.

Ollie finned over to her and stared at the find. He recognized the face as Hero and noticed the base of the statue firmly embedded in the sea floor. With a flash of inspiration he realized what Da Silva's clue "an HEROIC figure will point the way" meant. He signalled to the others to begin looking for more pieces.

If they could rebuild the statue of Hero, it would point towards the city.

In which direction should they swim?

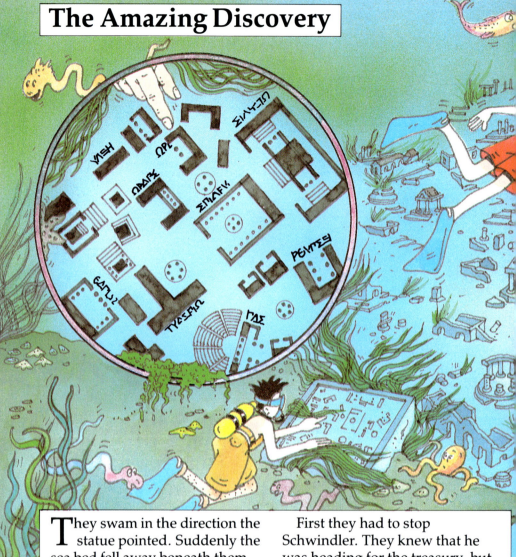

The Amazing Discovery

They swam in the direction the statue pointed. Suddenly the sea bed fell away beneath them. All four let out a gasp of air bubbles. Shimmering below were the ruins of an ancient city. There were great buildings made of marble blocks and glistening columns. They had found the sunken city. Toby turned a subaqua somersault, but there was no time to celebrate.

First they had to stop Schwindler. They knew that he was heading for the treasury, but where was it? Ollie quickly found the stone plan of the city mentioned by Da Silva. He brushed away the weeds and studied the writing. He soon found the treasury on the plan and pointed it out.

Which building is the treasury?

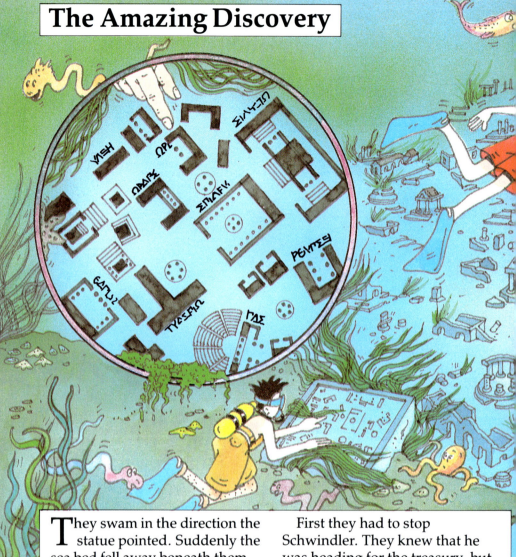

Subaqua Signals

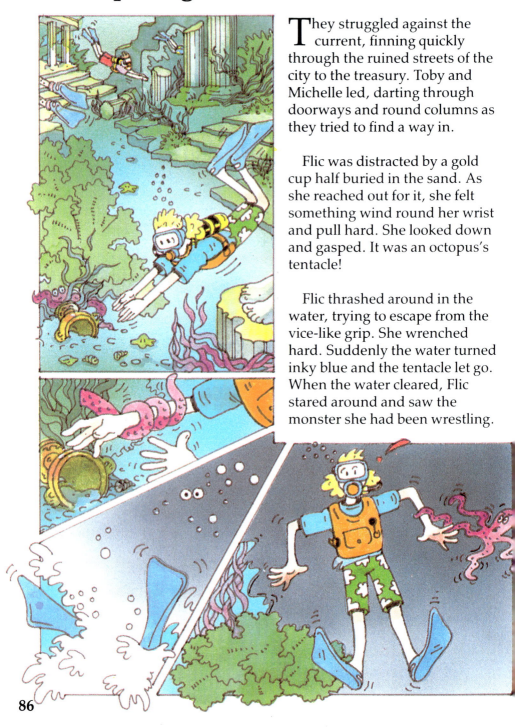

They struggled against the current, finning quickly through the ruined streets of the city to the treasury. Toby and Michelle led, darting through doorways and round columns as they tried to find a way in.

Flic was distracted by a gold cup half buried in the sand. As she reached out for it, she felt something wind round her wrist and pull hard. She looked down and gasped. It was an octopus's tentacle!

Flic thrashed around in the water, trying to escape from the vice-like grip. She wrenched hard. Suddenly the water turned inky blue and the tentacle let go. When the water cleared, Flic stared around and saw the monster she had been wrestling.

Feeling rather silly, she paddled through a marble arch to join the others. As they swam round to the front of the treasury, an electric eel curved past, almost touching Uncle Ollie.

Toby felt a hand grab his arm. Michelle pointed to Ollie who was waving his hands wildly at them. Why? Perhaps he was in trouble? Had he been shocked by the eel?

All of a sudden Toby realized what Ollie was doing. He was using his underwater sign language. But what was he trying to say? Ollie repeated his signals slowly.

What is Uncle Ollie saying?

A Desperate Plan

The trio spotted the danger immediately. Cruising through the submerged city was a mini-submarine . . with Schwindler at the helm.

At that moment the evil crook saw the divers. He snarled with anger and turned the mini-sub towards them. There was only one thing to do – swim for it.

They finned through the city, with Schwindler hard on their flippers. Flic glanced up and spotted a reef with a coral arch ahead. A desperate plan formed in her brain.

She signalled to the others and they swerved through the coral arch, closely followed by Schwindler. There was a nerve-jangling screech. The mini-sub was stuck fast.

Flic moved quickly.
As Schwindler tried to
back out of trouble,
Flic let off the signal
flare.

The Jolly Dodger
lowered a steel net.
Schwindler reversed
out of the arch and
into the trap.

He released the
ballast to try to escape
and the water frothed
with bubbles and
seaweed.

When the water cleared, Ollie,
Toby, Flic and Michelle watched
as the helpless villain and his
crew were hauled out of the water
to be clapped in irons.

Flic looked over to check her
oxygen and spotted something
that hadn't been visible before.

What has Flic noticed?

In the Throne Room

The four divers made their way through the clear water to explore the weed-covered building. They swam through the entrance and gasped at the magnificent room before them. They were inside the actual throne room of the sunken city.

Ollie was sure that the city was Mare Vellos, but he needed proof. And what about Da Silva? Had he really discovered it all those years ago? Suddenly Ollie spotted what he was looking for.

What has Ollie seen?

Clues

Pages 52-53
This is easy. Use your eyes.

Pages 54-55
Trace over the fragments of paper. Then piece them together.

Pages 58-59
Look carefully at Ollie's crew list. What are the crew saying?

Pages 60-61
You can see Da Silva's crest on page 56.

Pages 62-63
Port is left. Starboard is right.

Pages 64-65
Try thinking backwards.

Pages 66-67
First think of a word for a legal document about your last wishes. Then change the order of the letters in the word "mind" and put them into the middle of the word for a legal document.

Pages 68-69
They can jump over the gaps between rows of seats.

Pages 70-71
Write out the alphabet then substitute M for A, N for B, O for C and so on until A is substituted for O and finally L is substituted for Z.

Pages 72-73
Look carefully at what is on the ground.

Pages 74-75
Watch out for creepers with snakes on them.

Pages 76-77
Piece these fragments together with those on pages 54 and 55. Then check the map on page 63.

Pages 78-79
Where are Schwindler's plans?

Pages 80-81
Add up each column in turn. No number is repeated.

Pages 82-83
This is easy. Find all the pieces of the statue and put them together.

Pages 84-85
Compare the shape of the buildings in the city with the plan.

Pages 86-87
Check Ollie's underwater signals on page 59.

Pages 88-89
Keep your eyes peeled.

Page 90
Look back to pages 56 and 57.

Answers

Pages 52-53

This document is now missing from the room.

Pages 54-55

This is the document when pieced together. It is not complete because the thief has stolen the rest of the fragments.

> June 9th. The storm is over but we are badly damaged and off course. Our only chance is to make for land to carry out repairs and take on fresh supplies.
> June 10th. Sighted an uncharted group of islands. Dropped anchor and launched the jolly boat to explore. We first landed on a

> driven away by sheer numbers. We pushed off hurriedly. I steered our boat SW between a reef to port and three jagged rocks to starboard to an island with two hillocks at its centre. We left empty-handed, headed for the black island due S, swung SE to explore a half-sunken ship, then continued SE.

> covery. I left clues giving the location of the find on our island base.

The stolen diary fragments go here.

> skull-shaped isle, but it was barren of food and water so we rowed SE to a thickly wooded flat island. We found no water here and continued past foul-smelling seaweed to port towards an island due E. As we landed on the stony isle, thousands of red crabs scuttled angrily to attack. We roasted some but were

> We landed on the first island in our path and found fresh water, wild goats and plentiful wildfowl. We beached the Dolphin there.
> June 11th. The hull will take months to repair. The crew began building some huts, a windmill and a look-out post ...
> Aug 20th. An incredible day!! Have made the most amazing dis-

> top of the yellow rock to star-board, then dive.
> I sealed a chart of these islands in the sea chest bearing my crest and stowed it in my cabin aboard The Dolphin.

Pages 58-59

They can dive with Michelle Silver, the engineer. She is the only other experienced diver in the crew who can dive that day.

Ollie's dive details say that they each need one cylinder of air per dive. You can see the four full air cylinders ringed in the picture.

Pages 60-61

Toby has spotted the sea chest with Da Silva's crest.

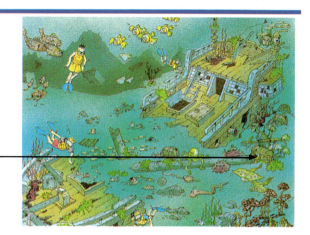

Da Silva's sea chest ——

Pages 62-63

Da Silva's route to his island base is described in the diary. It is marked here in black.

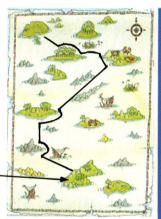

This was Da Silva's island base.

Pages 64-65

The message is written backwards with wrong spacings between words. This is what it says with punctuation added:

Oliver and the two brats must not, repeat not, search at the place where "a legal document about twisted mind is driven by natural forces". Otherwise they will find a vital message and clues hidden by Da Silva.

Pages 66-67

The place on the island is described with the cryptic clue: a place where "a legal document about twisted mind is driven by natural forces". Cryptic clues can be broken down into several parts which must be solved in turn. Words used in cryptic clues have their own special meaning. This cryptic clue is solved as follows:

1. A word meaning "a legal document" is **will**.

2. "About" is an instruction to place the word **will** around the solution to the next part of the clue.
3. "Twisted mind" is an instruction to change the order of the letters in the word **mind**.
4. To solve the clue, break the word **will** and put it on either side of the mixed up letters in the word **mind**. This produces the word **windmill**. This is a place "driven by natural forces".

Pages 68-69

The route up to the top of the amphitheatre is marked in black.

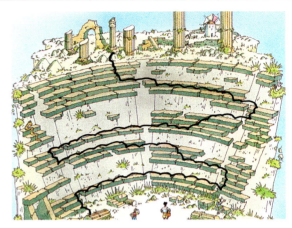

Pages 70-71

To decode the letters on the windmill sails write out the alphabet then substitute M for A, N for B, O for C, P for D, and so on through every letter of the alphabet.

To read the message, begin decoding the letters on the red sail, move round clockwise, then stop on the green sail. The rest is nonsense.

This is what the message says:

In the ruins out of sight of the windmill I left more clues to the location of the sunken city.

Pages 72-73

Flic has spotted a set of footprints on the ground that are identical to the thief's footprints on pages 54 and 55.

Flic has also spotted Ollie's magnifying glass.

Pages 74-75

They can tie one of the creepers to the rocks here.

Then they can climb down to these steps.

The rest of the route onto the boat is marked in black.

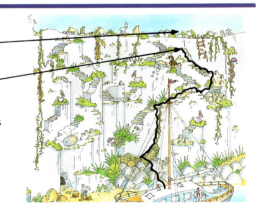

Pages 76-77

Schwindler's fragments of the diary (stolen by the thief on page 53) complete Da Silva's directions pinpointing the location of the sunken city.

To find out where to dive for the city, draw a straight line between the landmarks mentioned. The point where the two lines cross is where they should dive for the city.

have destroyed the ones I left earlier. Instead I took bearings to fix a definite point. Dive here and an HEROIC figure will show the way.
To find this point travel in a straight line from the northern-most tip of our island base towards the most eastern point on the wooded island with two

hills. When the summit of the highest peak on the black island to port aligns with the top of the yellow rock to star-board, then dive.
I sealed a chart of these islands in the sea chest bearing my crest and stowed it in my cabin aboard The Dolphin.

Dive here for the sunken city.

This fragment is in Toby and Flic's possession.

Pages 78-79

Schwindler's plans, which Toby saw through the porthole on page 76, prove that Schwindler intends to loot the city to make money for himself. He locked the plans in a drawer on page 77, but left the key in the cabin. To find the proof they must unlock the drawer.

The key

Pages 80-81

This is the limpet mine with all the buttons numbered correctly. To defuse the bomb they must press button number 13.

Pages 82-83

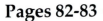

This is the intact statue.

Pages 84-85

When rebuilt, the statue points in the direction arrowed.

This building is the treasury.

Pages 86-87

You can see Ollie's signal chart on page 59. This is what he is saying.

Stop   Look   Left   Danger   Follow me

Pages 88-89

Flic has seen this building through the weeds.

Page 90

Ollie has spotted two things.

The crest on the throne is Hero's lion crest. You can see this on page 57. Mare Vellos shared the crest with Phabulos. This proves that the sunken city is Mare Vellos.

The telescope with Da Silva's crest proves that Da Silva must have discovered the city.

JOURNEY TO THE LOST TEMPLE

Susannah Leigh

Illustrated by John Blackman

Designed by Kim Blundell

Edited by Karen Dolby

Additional design and artwork by Christopher Gillingwater

Contents

About this Story

Journey to the Lost Temple is an exciting adventure story that takes you on a dangerous jungle trek in search of a fabulous lost temple.

Along the way, there are lots of tricky puzzles and perplexing problems which you must solve in order to understand the next part of the story.

Look at the pictures carefully and watch out for vital clues. Sometimes you will need to flip back through the book to help you find an answer. There are extra clues on page 139 and you can check the answers on pages 140-144.

Jack's and Em's adventure begins with a letter from their friend, Wanda.

Wanda

Veri Hotee
June 11 th

Dear Jack and Em,
Weather is hot, wish you were here - I need your help. Half of a priceless mask has been stolen from the city museum. Prime suspects are the Bruza Brothers, notorious art thieves. Now the mask's other half, hidden in the legendary lost temple, is in danger. It must be saved. The peace of Wat-A-Skor-Cha depends on it. Let me explain about the legend...

Jack   Em

Wanda Pharr is a famous explorer, working in the hot and hilly country of Wat-A-Skor-Cha. Turn the page to continue her letter.

The Legend of the Lost Temple

The story goes something like this...

Long ago, deep in the jungle of Wat-A-Skor-Cha, an ancient and wonderful temple was discovered. No one knew who had built it or why it was there. Inside was a room full of magnificent masks. One of them was made of a shimmery golden metal which glowed eerily in the darkness.. Its left eye was a priceless emerald and its right a perfect ruby...

Until then, the people of Wat-A-Skor-Cha had lived peacefully for hundreds of years. But the moment they saw the mask, a strange feeling came over each of them. They could not tear their eyes from its glow and each person's only wish was to possess the mask. They began arguing and a fierce struggle broke out. In the confusion there was an ear-splitting crack and the mask broke into two pieces.

At once there was silence. The people looked in terror at the two halves. The mask's glow had gone. Its spell was broken and the people no longer wanted to fight. But they knew if the mask were put together again its mysterious power would return and they were afraid.

So they decided to bring one half of the mask back to the town where it was kept in the museum. The right half with the ruby eye was left in the temple. This way its strange power would be controlled. Since that time the two halves have remained safely apart. The temple lies deep in the middle of the jungle but the way there has long been forgotten and the jungle is dangerous and deadly. Many have tried to find it, but none have returned...

Interesting story eh? I suspect the Bruza Brothers stole the mask from the museum and are now on their way to the temple to steal the ruby half of the mask as well. I can think of only one way to beat them. I must find the temple and retrieve its half mask before they do...Your puzzle-solving minds would be a great help.

Yours in desperation -Wanda xxx

Jack folded the letter. They had taken up Wanda's challenge and arrived in Wat-A-Skor-Cha. Their heads were buzzing with questions. Most important of all, Em wanted to find out more about the Bruza Brothers. All she knew was that they were ruthless crooks – cigar-smoking Bill Bruza and his slimy brother, Brian.

Now they had to meet Wanda. Below them was the valley of Veri-Hotee where she lived. Jack turned the envelope over to read the return address. Looking down at the huts again, he saw it was easy to work it out.

Which is Wanda's house?

FROM: Wanda Pharr
The Brown Hut
Tree View
Lakeside

Veri Hotel
W - A - S

AIRMAIL

AIRMAIL

Wanda Explains

Jack and Em peered through the door of Wanda's little house.

"Jack, Em!" she cried. "Come in. I'll tell you what's been going on."

"The night after the mask was stolen from the museum, an ancient map, showing the route back from the lost temple to Veri-Hotee, was taken from my hut," she explained. "I'm sure it was the Bruza's work again."

"The Bruzas haven't been seen since the break in," she continued. "They must be on their way to the temple . . . and the other half of the mask. When the mask is completed, they will hold its strange power and who knows what they will do with it then."

"Sounds a bit far-fetched to me," Jack said.

"I don't know if the legend is true," Wanda replied. "But the complete mask is priceless . . . a work of art. It musn't fall into the hands of the crooked Bruzas."

"So we MUST reach the temple before them," gasped Em. "But how do we get there without the map?"

"Well," began Wanda, sheepishly. "I believe there IS a copy of the map in the safe belonging to my predecessor, the esteemed travel writer, Ima Homesic. But the safe hasn't been opened for so long, I can't remember the combination."

"There must be a way into it," said Jack, peering at the dial.

"I THINK it's a six number sequence. It starts with a one," said Wanda, thinking hard. "And there's a four in there somewhere . . ."

"Then it's easy to work out," said Em.

What is the sequence that opens the safe?

The Mysterious Map

The dial clicked and the safe door swung open. Wanda lifted out a roll of yellowing parchment and spread it carefully on the table. Jack and Em stared at the ancient document.

There were strange pictures in circles joined by dotted lines.

"The red lines must show the route back from the temple," Wanda said.

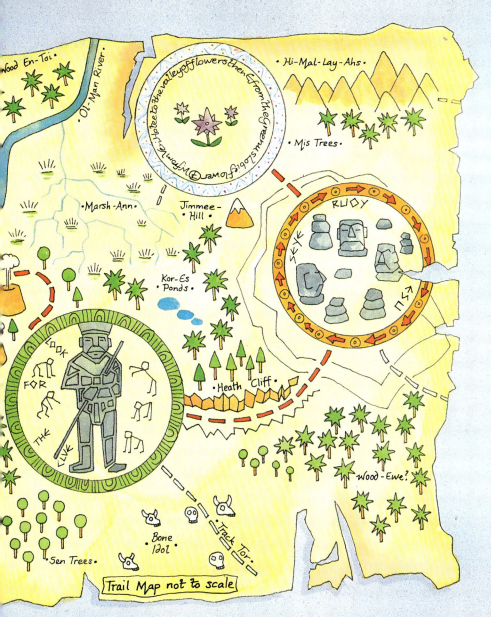

"I think the pictures are landmarks," she continued. "If each is found in the right order, they should lead to the temple."

"Where do we begin?" asked Em.

Jack looked at the circles and noticed some strange writing.

"I know what to do!" he said.

Do you?

The Journey Begins

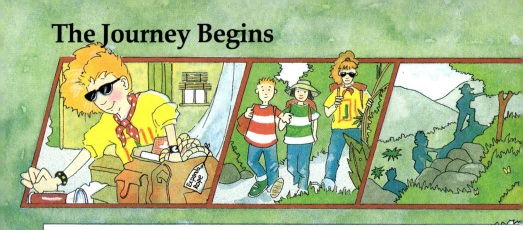

Early next morning, Wanda finally finished stuffing her explorer's back pack with all the handy equipment vital for their dangerous journey.

At last they set off. They climbed up into the wooded hills above the valley, away from the village, safety and civilization in search of the Greenus Lobie.

Further on, they came to a clearing in the middle of the jungle. Clusters of colourful flowers were dotted around.

"This must be it," said Wanda.

"But which flower is the right one?" asked Em.

"That's easy," Jack replied, as he pulled a dog-eared book on jungle plants from his back pack.

All around were tropical trees and bushes. There was no path and they had to fight their way through sharp bamboo and prickly shrubbery.

They were soon puffing and panting their way up a steep hill. The ground was stony and rocks crumbled and slipped beneath their feet.

Wat-A-Skor-Cha Flora

LOBUS BLUENESS
Long stemmed. Flowers may be purple, red or yellow. Tree loving.

LOBUS STINKUS
Indented leaves. Deadly poisonous. Flowers red from October to January and purple from February to September.

LOBUS FLUTTERBY
Purple or red flowers. Attracts butterflies.

GREENUS LOBIE
Indented leaves. Flowers purple October to December and red January to September. Harmless.

CREEPING LOBIE
Non-flowering climber. Grows up tree trunks.

LOBIE FLYTRAP
Red or yellow flowers. Eats insects. Indented leaves.

LOBUS SHADUS
Light blue flower. Tree and shade loving.

He turned to the right page and puzzled over the descriptions. Em and Wanda examined the flowers. It wasn't going to be so easy after all. Several of the flowers looked exactly the same.

Jack read his book carefully and looked very hard at the plants. Soon he was able to work it out.

Which is the Greenus Lobie?

Which Way?

Jack knelt down and put the compass directly above the clump of Greenus Lobie and took a bearing. Due east was a path through the forest.

"What's the next landmark?" asked Wanda, as they set off along the narrow path which twisted and turned through the thick jungle.

"Some strange stone heads," said Em, looking at the map.

Straight ahead through the trees, the three explorers caught sight of a small village with a few round huts.

As they drew nearer, several people came out to meet them. Em asked them for directions.

We're looking for some . . . er . . . stone heads. Do you know where they are?

OK. Go straight down till you see the jungle bar in front of you. Turn left and follow the path straight on. Second right and the path bends round to a small pool. Turn right and there they are. Easy.

That's not right. It's left from the village. Follow the path alongside the banana gro... It veers right, down some rock steps. Left, then right past the jungle bar. Right and left again, keep walking and you'll see the stones. Can't miss 'em.

No. You turn first right, then second left past the giraffes. The path divides, so go right and follow this route as it bends round. Um . . . under the bridge. Continue following the path round to the left and you're there.

The trio listened in dismay to the different directions. Which was the right route? Wanda couldn't work it out.

"There's only one thing for it." she sighed. "We'll take the first route. If that fails, we'll do the rest in order."

Jack and Em reluctantly agreed with her. They started off along the jungle path following the first set of instructions.

Where does the first route take them?
What about the other routes?

Message in the Stones

Five minutes and one deadly-looking snake pit later, Jack and Em began to wish that Wanda hadn't chosen the first route. But soon after, they were amazed and surprised to find they were where they wanted to be – at the strange stone heads.

"The power of the mask must be on our side," Wanda grinned.

The giant, carved heads stood in a large circle and were all different shapes. On the ground were broken bits of rock and stone. Em was puzzled. What was the secret of the heads? They certainly looked very sinister. Were they meant to search for an instruction or message? Perhaps the ancient map itself held the answer.

She sat down on a rock, took the map from her back pack and unrolled it. She read it carefully, hoping for inspiration. But without knowing what to look for, it wasn't easy. Suddenly it came to her in a flash, and looking at all the stones again, she quickly saw where to go next.

What has Em noticed?

Swamped!

The arrow directed the three explorers west. The shrieks and cackles of tropical birds and the calls of strange jungle animals echoed around them as they journeyed slowly along deep gulleys filled with strange shrubs and odd creatures. Suddenly they stopped. Directly in front of them was a large mangrove swamp.

"We'll never get across this," Jack groaned. "And we can't go round, the jungle's too thick."

"We could wade across," suggested Em, hopefully.

"No. It's too dangerous," Wanda replied. "That slime looks deep."

She pulled a long stick from the bank and plunged it into the marsh. It sank slowly, disappearing with a loud gurgle.

Jack shuddered as he thought of all the nasty things that might be lurking in the slime. He looked at the jungle surrounding the swamp and saw overhanging branches and thick creepers. A plan formed in his mind and he saw how to cross.

What is Jack's plan?

113

The Missing Clue

The swamp came to a shallow, sticky end. The trio struggled on ankle-deep in the murky water. Em led the way, trying to keep a sure footing as she followed the submerged path to firm ground. Flies buzzed noisily around Wanda's head as she ducked their angry attack. Meanwhile Jack felt a strange sensation on his arm. He looked down and saw leeches greedily slurping at his skin.

Deeper in the jungle, long vines hung down from the trees and swung in their faces, and scratchy thorn bushes grew close to the ground. Luckily, Wanda had remembered her handy jungle walking stick and they could cut their way through.

Jack began to feel very miserable. Sweat slowly trickled down his back and he wondered if they were heading in the right direction. It was getting hotter and hotter.

They stuck closely behind Wanda and when she stopped suddenly, Em and Jack tumbled over. As they picked themselves up from the ground, they saw a tall, stone plinth among the trees.

"The statue!" gasped Jack.

"Not any more," groaned Wanda, and she was right – the base was empty and the statue had gone.

"It could have been missing for centuries," Jack pointed out.

But Em was not so sure. Looking closely at the base of the statue, she knew it had been stolen very recently. And what's more, she could name the thieves.

What has Em spotted?
Who are the thieves?

All Tied Up

Suddenly Em felt a hand on her shoulder. She spun round quickly to find herself face to face with a large, round-faced man. He wore a big hat and from his thin mouth dangled a fat cigar. He was very scary.

"Gotcha!" snarled Bill Bruza. "But unfortunately for you, this is the last puzzle you'll be solving for a very long time."

"Maybe forever," giggled his slimy brother, Brian.

Jack gulped. He had heard so much about the evil pair, but he'd never imagined they would look so villainous. He shivered as the gruesome twosome circled slowly around them.

Brian Bruza tied the trio's hands and Bill pushed them roughly on into the dark jungle. The captives stumbled and tripped over the bumpy ground until they came to a group of tall trees.

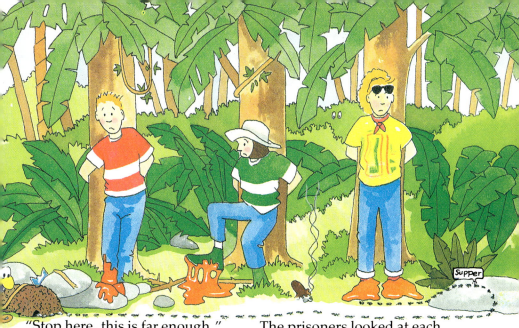

"Stop here, this is far enough," growled Bill as he tied Wanda, Jack and Em to three sturdy trees. "This is where your journey ends."

"If the wild animals don't eat you first, you'll starve," Brian cackled, following his brother away into the jungle.

The prisoners looked at each other in despair. Was this the end? They shivered in spite of the heat as the same thought crossed their minds. Were they to be lion food that night? They tried to struggle free, but it was useless. Their hands seemed to be firmly tied.

How can they escape?

Crossing the Crocodile Creek

Jack tugged at his ropes – a quick release knot! He wriggled his hands free.

"Those Bruzas need a lesson in knot tying," he laughed, as he unknotted the cords around Wanda's and Em's wrists.

In the distance they could hear running water and in a flash Wanda remembered the map. It must be the waterfall! They set off at a run in the direction of the noise. Soon they arrived at a grassy bank. Across the river was the waterfall. Stepping stones and logs made a path to the other side of the bank.

"Let's cross here!" said Jack, about to hop onto the first log.

"Watch out!" cried Em. "It's not a log, it's a crocodile!"

Swiftly Jack jumped back. Em was right. And now Jack saw that some of the stones looked like hippos. They even had flies buzzing around them.

"What do we do now?" he asked.

"Follow me," said Wanda. "I think I can see a way across."

Can you find a safe route across the river avoiding the watery creatures?

119

The Waterfall Surprise

They scrambled onto the rocky shore. The waterfall crashed and cascaded around them and spray from the water splashed their faces.

"What next?" yelled Em, above the roar of the fall.

"This is useless," Jack moaned, sitting down glumly on a rock. "How can this waterfall lead us to the temple?"

"We can't give up now," said Wanda. "We've got to find the temple before the Bruzas. They must be way ahead of us."

"Perhaps we'll be able to see from the top," said Em, beginning to climb the rocks at the side of the fall. Wanda was right behind.

Reluctantly Jack followed them. He was feeling very miserable and hungry, and his boots were full of water. But the climb was easier then it looked. There were handy foot holds in the rock.

Just then Em caught sight of something amazing. This could be what they were looking for.

"Look over there," she yelled.

They inched themselves across to investigate and saw a narrow gap between two boulders. Jack and Wanda could hardly believe their eyes when they peered through the hole and saw a rocky staircase, ending in darkness. Jack felt excited as they slipped between the rocks and crept down the steps.

At the bottom was a dimly-lit chamber. Rocks grew from the roof and floor. But there was nothing else to see. The trail seemed to have run dry. Now it was Em's turn to feel glum.

"It's a dead end," she said.

Jack was leaning against the wall when he gave a shout.

"Look at this!" he yelled and pointed to a small wooden lever sticking out from a stone slab. Eagerly he tugged it.

WHOOSH! There was a rushing sound and the floor gave way. Their stomachs dropped as they fell down and down a rocky chute. CRASH. They landed at the bottom in the gloomy darkness.

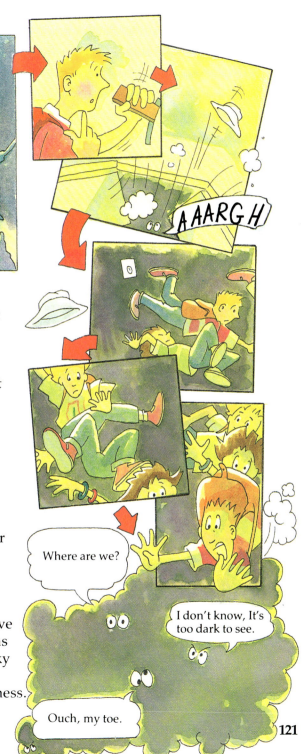

Cryptic Code

There was silence followed by a soft rustling sound. Jack shivered and Em's skin tingled.

"Its only me," said Wanda cheerfully. "I'm looking for the torches in my back pack."

Em wished she would hurry. It was dark and creepy in the cave. The sound of dripping water came from far away and strange creatures squeaked in the silence. At last Wanda handed her a torch and she clicked it on.

"Come on," Wanda said. "We've got to work out where to go now."

Her voice trailed away as she shone the torch into the inky blackness and gasped at what she found there.

Dead ahead was a rock face. Carved into it was a square frame. It was covered with rows and rows of strange symbols.

"What is it?" whispered Jack, peering at the squiggles.

"It's an old Wat-A-Skor-Cha cypher," Wanda replied. "They were used by the ancient people for very secret messages. There were lots of different ones."

"Amazing!" she continued. "It's the cypher I was studying before we left. I have my notes with me."

She showed Em and Jack her work, but it wasn't complete.

"If we fit the letters to the symbols shown here, the rest of the message might fall into place," said Em thoughtfully.

What do the symbols say?

Jumbled Jigsaw

The cypher said their goal was getting closer, but first they had to find the green crystals. They were just wondering which way to turn when Em spotted a small, narrow passageway at the back of the cave. She squeezed through to investigate.

"In here!" she called, her voice echoing through the hollow cave.

Jack and Wanda speedily followed her. They found themselves in a large, round cavern. Shadows lengthened on the walls and water dripped slowly from the cracked rock. But the cool air was refreshing after the hot, sticky jungle.

"Quick. Over here with the torch," Em called.

She was standing by the far wall of the cavern. From a distance it looked rough and worn. But there was something interesting about it . . .

In the torchlight they saw that it was covered with strange pictures, but there were also gaps in the wall where the bare rock showed through.

At their feet lay pieces of stone with more pictures painted on them. They came from the spaces in the wall where the rock had crumbled away.

"Maybe it's another clue." said Em. "Perhaps we should work out where these pieces fit in."

What does the painting show?

Elephant Walk

It was exciting to see the temple in pictures, but they hadn't learnt anything new. At that moment their attention was distracted by a shining light in the corner of the cave . . . the green crystals! They hurried over and scrabbled through the glowing rocks. But the key wasn't there.

"The Bruzas have beaten us to it!" groaned Em.

"Then we must hurry to catch up with them," Wanda said.

Jack spotted a small gap in the roof above them. Cut into the walls were foot and hand holds.

Breathless, the three scrambled out of the cave, onto a high, rocky plateau. The land around was desert-like, but in the distance the jungle started again. Wanda pulled her binoculars from her back pack and tried to get her bearings.

Suddenly she gasped. Far away was a tiny dot. Hardly daring to believe her eyes, Wanda peered through the lenses. At last . . . the temple! It was just visible through the distant tree tops. They set the compass and began their final trek.

The sun beat down as they crossed the plain. Just when they thought they could go no further, Wanda spotted three hefty elephants. She remembered the map.

"Let's hitch a lift," she said.

She gently tapped one on its front knee. The elephant knelt down and Wanda climbed onto his back.

"It's OK," she said. "I'm an expert at this."

Jack and Em did the same. And at a word from Wanda, the strange procession set off.

Em was surprised to find the ride so uncomfortable, but it was better than walking. Soon they had left the desert and were trekking into jungle again. They climbed down from the elephants and left them at a pool, then walked on through the trees.

Suddenly they stopped. They were at the edge of a high cliff – and far below was the temple. Would they ever reach it? They HAD to find a way down the cliff. Then Wanda had a brainwave.

How can they get down?

127

The Temple

Their pulses raced as they neared their final goal. Suddenly there it was, tall and imposing . . . the lost temple. Ancient stone statues lined the path to the heavy doors and carved faces glared down at them. Creepers had grown over the temple walls, but it was still magnificent. They had arrived.

"But it's no good," said Jack, staring at the temple. "We don't have the key to get in."

Em marched up to the heavy iron doors. She heaved and pushed with all her might, but they wouldn't budge. She peered through the keyhole and saw nothing but blackness.

"We're too late," she wailed. "The Bruzas must have locked the door behind them. Now the whole mask is in their power and it will never belong to Wat-A-Skor-Cha again."

"We can't give up now after all we've been through," said Wanda. "There must be another way in."

But they found no other door. Their brains whirred. What was their next move? Em looked in frustration at the temple again. It was then that she remembered something important. If her hunch was right there was another way inside.

How can they get into the temple?

Monkey Business

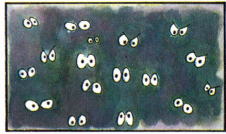

Em climbed the statue and with a great tug, turned the head around. There was a grating sound and a small panel in the side of the temple slid open. Cautiously they stepped through into the dark. To his horror, Jack saw hundreds of pairs of eyes staring back at him.

"Someone else is here," gasped Wanda. "Switch on the torch."

WHOOSH. A small, brown, furry creature swung past Em's ear. The room was full of chattering monkeys, swinging from creepers and hanging from the walls.

They scanned the room and quickly realized the mask wasn't there. They walked on into a cold, narrow corridor which curved round to the right.

Statues lined the walls. The passage ended and they turned right into a wider corridor, left past a snake mosaic and then first right.

Next left was a dead end, but it led them to a plan of the temple. In the centre was a mask. This HAD to be the mask room they were looking for.

Jack tried to remember their route so far.

Where are they now? How can they get to the mask room?

The Bruzas Return

Minutes later they reached the room at the centre of the temple. It was filled with masks. Some were whole, but most were broken.

But there was no time to look for the temple's ruby-eyed half mask. At that moment they heard footsteps and familiar voices behind them.

It was the Bruza Brothers. Bill snarled gruffly at slimy Brian, who giggled. Then they stared menacingly at the trio who were cornered again.

Bill lunged for Jack but he dived through Bill's legs. Wanda tripped Brian who went flying. Then Em spotted something in Bill's bag and a desperate plan formed in her head. It was their only chance . . .

She grabbed a creeper and with a yell, swung from it, aiming for Bill's bag. A direct hit! Before bewildered Bill knew what was happening, the emerald-eyed mask had catapulted from his bag.

It fell through the air. With a sickening thud it landed beside Jack who tried not to worry about the way the mask was being thrown about. Bungling Brian dived to grab it, but Jack got there first.

Jack threw the mask to Wanda just as Brian reached him. Now it was Wanda's turn to dodge the slimy pair. Falling over themselves in their desperate attempts to grab the mask, the Bruzas stumbled towards Wanda.

Swiftly she dodged the crooks and running around behind them, quickly passed the mask to Em, who was hiding behind a large statue. The Bruzas were dizzy. They just weren't quick enough to outwit the trio.

Over here, I've got a plan!

But Jack, Em and Wanda were tiring. They had to escape with the mask, but how? As they dodged the Bruzas' evil clutches, Jack had a feeling he had seen this room somewhere before.

He thought over what he had learned about the temple so far. Then he realized the room held the secret to trapping the Bruzas. If he could only find the lever . . . He grabbed the mask and ran.

He reached the corner of the room, both Bruzas in hot pursuit. Jack spun round to dodge them. The brothers collided and Jack darted across to the wall.

What is Jack's plan?

133

The Missing Mask

Jack speedily yanked a rusty handle and there was a loud, whirring sound. Before the Bruzas had time to pick themselves up, a heavy wooden grid crashed down across a corner of the room. The Bruzas were trapped behind it.

"Good work," grinned Wanda. "We'll have to trek to the nearest village for help with the crooks."

Jack held the half mask that the Bruzas had stolen from the museum and looked at it closely for the first time. Its emerald eye winked back at him.

"We must find its other half," Em said. "Don't forget the cypher."

The room was full of relics. There were statues, idols and hundreds of broken masks. Finding the right half seemed impossible. Then, out of the corner of her eye, Wanda saw something shining. If the old legend about the mask was right, she had found its other half, left in the temple for centuries.

Where is the temple's half mask?

The Temple Remains

Carefully, Wanda held both halves of the mask in her hands. Jack and Em watched with bated breath as Wanda hesitated, wondering whether she should put it back together.

All of a sudden there was a bright flash and the mask jumped out of Wanda's hands. As if by magic, it was whole again. The ground shook and a shower of rocks fell from the ceiling.

"Lets get out of here!" cried Em. "The roof's caving in."

But a frightened shout made her turn around quickly. The Bruzas were still trapped. Quickly Jack pushed the lever. The grill slid up and the Bruzas raced away. They sped out of the temple with petrified yells.

The temple was collapsing fast. Stone slabs crashed down around them. Em and Wanda dashed to the door and on through the maze of corridors to the temple's exit. Jack was right behind, but stopped to look back at the mask. It was shaking and glowing. Jack shuddered and sprinted out just before the roof gave way.

He reached the safety of the jungle just in time. There was a final loud crack as the temple disappeared in a cloud of dust. Coughing and spluttering, Wanda, Em and Jack stared speechless at the ruins.

"The mask was more powerful than we thought," gasped Em finally. "But at least no one can take it now. It's vanished for ever."

Or has it?

What Happened Next . . .

Daily Skorcha – July 20th

FETE SUCCESS

The annual Wat-A-Skor-Cha orphanage garden fete on Saturday was a grand success, raising a lot of money for charity. In particular, the tombola was a great favourite with the excited crowds. The fete was ceremoniously opened by Mr Bill Bruza, the orphanage's newly appointed head governor.

SHADY DEALS

His appointment came as some surprise to those who know of his former activities in the world of petty theft and shady deals. However his recent, and very generous, foray into the world of children's charities has shown his sincerity to reform.

SUPERNATURAL

We asked Bill why he had given all his money to charity, and where his brother and ex-partner in crime, Brian was. Mr Bruza's reply was very vague. He hinted at strange supernatural experiences and some children who'd saved his life. "My brother Brian?" Bill concluded. "He's taken a very long holiday in the Caribbean."

'Wat-A-Skor-Cha World' July 22nd

TEMPLE UPDATE

Many explorers have tried – and failed – to follow the trail to the lost temple, first blazed by local girl, explorer Wanda Pharr, and her two young assistants Jack and Em. Wanda, who made her intrepid journey last month heroically prevented the fabulous mask of the temple from falling into the hands of two villainous thieves.

MYSTERIOUS

After a reported earthquake destroyed the temple, the mask disappeared under the ruins. However, it was never clear if the mask really had been lost for ever.

CHANCE DISCOVERY

Further light was shed on this question recently when a group of botanists, led by the distinguished scientist, Teresa Green, stumbled upon the ruined temple. Ms Green and her party had lost their way in the jungle while searching for the rare Orchid Narcotica plant, when they made their chance discovery of the Lost Temple.

Teresa Green

SWALLOWED UP

"We spotted the famous mask glinting among the rubble," Ms Green told us exclusively. "One of my team reached out to grab it. At the same moment the earth shook and began to crack. There was a roar of thunder, although it was a clear day. Then sparks flew – it was really spooky. We jumped back just in time. The ground in front of us opened up and swallowed the temple, mask and all. With a final shudder it closed again. There was nothing left at all of the Lost Temple."

THE TRUTH? Ed's comment.

There is no doubt that the story of the lost temple and its fabulous mask is a strange one. Could there be some truth in the old legend about the mask's strange powers after all? Surely not, although perhaps you should make up your own minds . . .

from 'The Skorch' July 26th

Brian Bruza

BRIAN BRUZA'S BOPPER

Crazy about dancing? Crazy about having a good time? Just plain crazy? Nip over to the island of Ripee-Offee in the Caribbean and experience the magic and lights of a dynamite Disco – **BRIAN BRUZA'S BOPPER**. Truly a night to remember.

★First night party **MASKED BALL!**★

Clues

Answers

Pages 100 – 101

Wanda's address describes
the location of her house.

This is Wanda's house

Pages 102 – 103

The combination that opens the safe
is 1,4,7,10,13,16. The numbers form a sequence, with the numbers
increasing by three each time.

Pages 104 – 105

Jack has realized the circled
landmarks have clues written around
them. The flower picture is marked
number 7. The temple is marked
number 1. This suggests that the trail
runs backwards from the temple to
the village. There are only seven
circled landmarks, so the flower
picture is the first clue on the trail
from Veri-Hotee. The writing around
it is in a continuous line. With spacing
added it says: W(est) from Veri Hotee
to the valley of flowers. Then E(ast)
from the Greenus Lobie flower.
The words around the stone heads
are written backwards. They say: Use
your eyes.
The writing around the elephants is
also backwards. It says: You're on the
right trail.
The messages on the crocodile and
waterfall pictures are in mirror
writing. They say: Keep going, and:
Don't give up.

Pages 106 – 107

There is only one plant that fits the
description of the Greenus Lobie in
the book. As the month is June (see
Wanda's letter on page 99), the book
tells you the Greenus Lobie's petals
are red.

The Greenus Lobie is ringed in black.

Pages 108 – 109

In fact, all the routes lead to the stones, they just follow different paths. Each is marked in the picture.

KEY:

Route A ————

Route B ————

Route C ————

Pages 110 – 111

Em has noticed a stone arrow. It has the same markings as the border around the stone head picture on the map.

Here is the arrow ⟶

Pages 112 – 113

This is Jack's plan:

1) Using the branches, they climb up this tree.

6) They walk along this branch to the shore.

2) They inch along this branch and drop down to this small island.

5) They can then use this stepping stone to reach the tree trunk.

3) They break off this forked stick and use it to hook the creeper.

4) Next they swing across to this island.

Pages 114 – 115

Em has spotted three things:

1. Creepers which cover the plinth have not yet grown over the spot where the statue stood, suggesting it has been stolen recently.
2. There are fresh footprints leading up to and away from the plinth that don't match the pattern of Jack's,

Em's and Wanda's shoes. (You can see the underside of their shoes on page 114.) This suggests someone has been here just before them.

3. There is a smouldering cigar in the bushes. Em knows that Bill Bruza smokes a cigar, and so she concludes that the Bruzas are the thieves.

Pages 116 – 117

Jack's hands have only been tied with a quick release knot. If he pulls the end of the rope, the knot will come undone easily. The ropes around Wanda's and Em's hands are more securely tied.

Pages 118 – 119

The safe route across the river is marked in black.

Pages 122 – 123

To decode the cypher, first change all the symbols marked in Wanda's notebook to their corresponding letter, e.g. ◁ =A and / =I etc. When you have done this, you should be able to work out the rest of the letters to make up the words.

Here is the message decoded, with punctuation added:

The temple gates are locked you will see
But under green crystals in this cave is th
key.
If all else fails and the key you cannot fir
Turn the head that looks behind.
But a warning to all who enter that place
If you have in your hands the emerald-eyed face,
It must be rejoined with its ruby-eyed mate –
This action alone seals the temple's fate.

Pages 124 – 125

This is what the picture looks like when complete. It shows the ancient people journeying back from the temple.

Pages 126 – 127

Wanda has a rope in her back pack (see page 106). If they tie it to the sturdy rock at the top of the cliff, they can use it to scramble down.

Pages 128 – 129

Em spots that this statue's head is facing the wrong way.
She remembers the line from the cryptic message in the cave (pages 122 to 123), "if all else fails . . . turn the head that looks behind". She realizes this must be the head it is referring to.

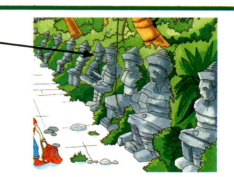

Pages 130 – 131

The route they have just taken is marked in black. The way to the mask room is marked in green.

They started here

Pages 132 – 133

Jack has seen the room before in the wall painting on pages 124 to 125. From this, he knows that when the lever on the wall is pulled a grill falls down, cutting off a corner of the room to protect the mask. He realizes that if he lures the Bruzas to this corner of the room, he can trap them behind the grill.

Pages 134 – 135

Here is the mask's other half.

The legend says that the mask's left half has an emerald eye, and its right a ruby eye. Jack is holding the emerald half. This means they have to look for the mask's right half with the ruby eye.

Pages 136 – 137

You can just see the mask poking out from under the rubble. Here it is.

First published in 1990 by
Usborne Publishing Ltd,
Usborne House, 83-85 Saffron Hill,
London EC1N 8RT, England.

Copyright © 1990 Usborne Publishing Ltd.

The name Usborne and the device 🪂 are Trade Marks of Usborne Publishing Ltd.

Printed in Belgium